The Little Mermaid

Fairy Tale Classics
STORYBOOK

Once upon an ocean tide,
in the deepest waters,
lived a wise and mighty Sea King
who had some mermaid daughters.

The youngest was his favorite girl,
lovely, kind and fair.
She only longed to see the world
of men and ships and air.

So when the mermaid turned fifteen,
she finally got her wish,
that she could see what lay beyond
the coral reefs and fish.

Alone one night away from home,
she watched ships come and go.
On one she saw a handsome Prince
and her heart began to glow.
But suddenly, some lightning flashed
and struck the ship below!

Waves crashed down upon the deck
amidst the roaring thunder.
The mighty sails were torn in two;
the ship was going under!

The Little Mermaid saved the Prince
and pulled him safe to shore.
And while he slept she sang to him
for half an hour, maybe more.

Soon the Little Mermaid heard
the sound of someone near.
She hid herself behind a rock,
just close enough to hear.

A maiden came upon the Prince
and told him to awake.
He did, and said, "You saved my life!
A perfect wife you'll make."
So with the maiden he then went,
oh, what a sad mistake!

The Little Mermaid's heart was crushed,
and all her dreams were dashed.
But now she knew what mattered most:
"It's love!" and off she splashed.

The Little Mermaid thought aloud,
"I have to meet the Prince."
So to the Sea Witch she did swim,
For legs instead of fins.

The Witch said, "Yes, I'll give you legs
so you can walk on land.
And in exchange, your lovely voice
is all that I demand!"

The Little Mermaid nodded while
the Sea Witch poured her potion.
And bravely did she gulp it down,
so she could leave the ocean.

And quicker than a white-whale wink,
her graceful mermaid flippers
were transformed into human legs,
her feet in purple slippers!

And there she stood up on the shore,
her new knees getting weak.
The Prince rode by and said hello.
Alas! She could not speak!

The Prince could not explain it, but
the Little Mermaid's smile
made his heart feel ten times lighter than
it had for quite a while.

The Prince then told his bride-to-be,
"I've brought a guest to stay."
To this she said, "It seems your friend
has nothing much to say!"

And feeling rather jealous of
the Little Mermaid's beauty,
she added, "Entertaining guests
is NOT a prince's duty."

But every night the Prince did take
the Little Mermaid walking.
Of course, she could not say a word,
so he did all the talking.

One day, the bride-to-be did say,
"Let's get just one thing clear—
Once the Prince and I are wed,
you won't be welcome here!"

The Little Mermaid cried and cried
and ran down to the sea.
She wondered if she was better off
than the way she used to be.

Not knowing that the Prince was there
and watching all along,
the Little Mermaid jumped when he
reached out and said, "What's wrong?"

Of course, she could not tell him so,
but love had filled her eyes
and deeply touched the Prince's heart,
for true love never lies.

Now maybe it was magic true,
no one can ever tell,
but when the Prince gave her a kiss
it broke the Witch's spell!

When suddenly the Mermaid sang,
the young Prince finally knew.
"You're the one who rescued me!
I owe my life to *you.*

"Please forgive my foolishness,
I made a hasty choice."
The Little Mermaid sighed, "My Prince,"
in her strong and lovely voice.

The wedding day arrived at last;
the bells rang out at dawn.
(In search of other wealth and fame,
the maiden was long gone.)

And as the Prince embraced his new
and lovely bride-to-be,
she said, "My Prince, my love for you
is deeper than the sea."

And in the distance, they could hear
the Sea King's gentle laughter,
which was his way of wishing them,
a happy ever after.